by Jo Brown

Where's My Mommy?

tiger tales

One day a large egg rolled out of a nest, down a hill, and landed at the bottom with a CRACK!

With a push and a shove, a small
green head popped out. It was a
baby crocodile.
"Where's my mommy?" he asked.

Little Crocodile looked around and saw a monkey hanging from a branch.

"Are you my mommy?" Little Crocodile asked.

"Well, can you swing from a tree like me?"
asked the monkey.

Little Crocodile
couldn't even reach the
lowest branch.
"And can you do this?" said the monkey...

E E EEE AAA

Little Crocodile tried, but all
that came out of his mouth was . . .

Snap

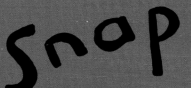

"No, you're definitely not a
monkey," said the monkey. "But I'm
sure you'll find your mommy soon."
So Little Crocodile wandered off
along the path.

He met an elephant splashing around in the water.

"Hello," said Little Crocodile.
"Are you my mommy?"

UUUU

Snap

Little Crocodile tried, but all that
came out of his mouth was . . .

"Well, you're definitely
not an elephant," said the
elephant. "Keep looking
for your mommy."

So Little Crocodile walked on
in search of his mommy.

He came across a tiger lazing in the sun.

"Hello there," said Little Crocodile politely. "Are you my mommy?"

"Well, can you roll around in
the grass like me?" asked the tiger.

"Yes!" said Little Crocodile, but he kept getting stuck . . .
upside down.

"And can you do this?"
asked the tiger.

OOOARR

Little Crocodile tried, but all
that came out of his mouth was...

Snap

The tiger definitely wasn't
his mommy. So Little Crocodile
plodded on.

He met a zebra munching some grass.

"Are you my mommy?"
asked Little Crocodile
hopefully.

"Well, can you kick your back legs high up in the air like me?" replied the zebra.

Little Crocodile tried but it was no use.

"And can you do this?"

AYYY HEY HEY

Little Crocodile tried,
but all that came out
of his mouth was... **Snap**

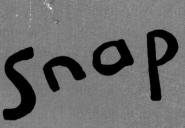

"No, you're definitely not a zebra," said
the zebra. "But don't be upset. I will help
you find your mommy. Hop on my back!"
And off they went.

Before long, they arrived at the river where Little Crocodile saw ...

lots of
splashing.

"I think I can do that!" said Little Crocodile, smiling...

and he could!
"And can you do this?" asked
the other crocodiles…

as they dived in the water with their tails in the air.

"Sure," said Little Crocodile.
"And can you do this?" asked
the other crocodiles.

Yes he could! **Snap**

"Oh, there you are!" said Mommy Crocodile, "I've been looking for you everywhere." She gave Little Crocodile a big smile. "Where have you been?"

"Oh, just making a few friends," said Little Crocodile.